Love or Lies?

Evincepub
Publishing

Evincepub Publishing

Parijat Extension, Bilaspur, Chhattisgarh 495001

First Published by Evincepub Publishing 2018

ISBN: 978-1-5457-1664-9

Price: Rs.199/-

Love or Lies?

Aisha Shaikh

About The Book

Love, lies, betrayal.

He flirted? She's hurt, He lied? She cried.

He promised? She kept it, He loved her? Now she knew it was a lie.

Based on 3 real life stories with 3 different couples.

Secrets and lies kill love, no matter how careful the player is, he gets caught.

Stories about a "guy" wanting his wife to sleep with his best friend.

Another "using" an innocent girl to get back his ex.

The last one having affairs with random girls whenever he fought with his girlfriend, during the process to get her back & also when he got her back.

Are you with anyone of them or ARE YOU ONE OF THEM?

About The Author

Aisha Shaikh has completed her Bachelors in Media Science, now pursuing her masters. She is also a blogger.

She has inculcated the habit of writing since childhood when she would write to several big MNCs like ITC, Dabur, Procter & Gamble etc. commenting on the products they deliver and always received huge gift hampers and letters from their CEOs as an acknowledgement since she was in fourth standard.

She also wrote to Late Dr A.P.J Abdul Kalam Azad (Former President of India) and got a reply from him personally.

As an author this is her first book, with other novels already lined up for publication.

Connect with her on her page at -

www.facebook.com/aisha1shaikh

1. ARJUN AND ADITI

1.1

Arjun was a well-established software engineer working in Ireland. He was good-looking, charming, soft-spoken and composed. He was introduced to me by a friend at a party. We went to many road trips, movies, restaurants, functions with friends. He had come to India to attend his sister's wedding. He went back after a few days and we kept in touch through phone. Our first conversation after he left -

"Hi Aditi"

"Hi Arjun, how are you doing?"

"Already missing someone."

"Who?"

"You" he laughed.

I started laughing too but it felt good hearing this from him.

We spoke a lot, almost daily, after his and my office hours. We enjoyed speaking to each other and I started missing him more and more as each day passed.

Suddenly he stopped calling for a week. I thought maybe he has started dating somebody, that's why he is keeping busy. Come on, that's what every girl thinks. If not me, then definitely somebody else was keeping him busy.

He sent me lots of pictures of his office, new home, new car and said he was busy with all these. For me, there was no way to believe him. Definitely, someone else was having his attention. But he wanted to speak so we spoke like before. Even I wanted to speak to him. I enjoyed his company.

1.2

"How have you been Aditi?"

"Fine, you?"

"I missed you Aditi"

"I missed you too"

"It's my friend's birthday party tonight, what should I wear?"

"Remember the blue shirt we bought together?" I asked

"Yes, I will wear that."

"Have fun there"

"I will call you once I get back"

But he did not call for 2 days. I started getting upset and missing him even more. Why was he giving me such gaps? Whenever he called again after a break he made me feel as if I was the most important woman in his life. He always made me smile, made me feel special and wanted.

One day he said, "My flatmate tried to kill me."

I was scared for him and asked, "Why? What happened?"

"He has split personality disorder, he is like the best buddy at times but when his another personality takes over, he thinks everyone or anyone around him is trying to kill him but in reality they are not and in his defense, he attacks with anything he gets hold of."

"That's really scary, did he hurt you?"

"No, I just shifted from there."

"Why didn't you inform the police?"

"I didn't want to."

"Okay."

We loved talking to each other, I was falling in love with him, he took care of me really well. He asked me about everything, always showed concern-whether I had dinner, what I had, if I was taking my vitamins on time, how my new office was, if there was any difficulty at my workplace-with my colleagues or boss. He cared way too much about me and he kept giving me hints of how amazing it would be if we were a couple.

I was just waiting for him to propose me. His getting disappeared for days was very annoying and that kept me away from giving him hints too otherwise I would have said I like him, or even more than that. I wanted him with me full time, not half time, spare time or sometimes.

I often asked him what kept him away for days but he always came up with not so believable excuses. I had many friends proposing me at my office, but I kept saying no to them. My heart wanted Arjun. I had fallen for him and I was waiting for him to fall for me too.

1.3

"Aditi, I want to see you."

"Me too"

"Come on skype."

"Received it"

"You look amazing."

"You look handsome."

He showed me around his flat, his new flatmate was out of town. It was a nice house, his room was just perfectly set. I thought it would be like other bachelor pads which are more like a garbage dumping site. But he didn't look like that either, he was always organised, disciplined and hard working.

"You know Aditi, sometimes I feel so lonely here."

"But you have so many friends."

"They are my friends, always busy with their own lives."

"You guys hang around a lot as compared to many guys who are staying away from home"

"I know but you are not understanding"

"Try"

"Someone who I can count upon always, somebody I know who is waiting back at home for me and I have to rush from office to see her like all my married friends do" he smiled and said.

I was getting little happy from within. I was waiting for him to say something like this.

"Aditi I love you. I really mean it. We have not spent time together alone but I really enjoy talking to you."

"I like talking to you as well", I said but I wanted to say - I love you too idiot, do you even know how long I have been waiting to hear this. But I controlled my happiness and looked back at him.

"Marry me", he said.

"I don't know what to say", I said when I very well knew what to say. I wanted to jump and say yes yes yes. But again I composed myself.

"I am coming to see you."

WOW!

"When?", I asked.

"Next month."

"But you were supposed to come back after 8 months."

"No, I am taking a leave of 5 days and I am just coming to see you. I won't go home, I won't even say that I have come to India or else they will demand half of the time. I want to spend these 5 days with you to give you the opportunity to know me better and say yes for marriage."

"That's nice."

"I am already ready for you Aditi, I don't need time to decide, I just want you to know me better and fall in love with me."

I didn't sleep all night. Each and every word of his was repeating on my mind. I really wanted him to know that I love him but the idea of him coming to me and spending time wanted me to withdraw from confessing my love to him.

We spoke regularly for a week, this time with more depth and affection. He made me fall for him with every word which came out from his mouth, hours passed just like that, I had no track of time when I spoke to him.

But again he was out of contact for 3 weeks. I was really mad at him. We messaged each other at times. I never called him first, it was him who always initiated every conversation. I hated him for staying away for that long.

1.4

"Aditi, I am coming to see you in 3 days."

"Where were you?"

"Working for you."

"Do you work 24*7?"

"Yes, I was working overtime."

"But that doesn't mean you couldn't take out even 10 minutes a day for me."

"Baby, I am sorry!"

Again he didn't call me for the remaining 3 days. I didn't want to speak to him ever. Neither did I want to meet him now. It was really weird of him to make me feel like I am his world and then disappear for days.

If somebody is really into you, not a single moment will pass without thinking of that special someone. I would think of him every moment, I longed to speak to him whenever I had free time, I always checked my phone even while working at the office to see whether there was any call from him.

My waiting and his disappearing was a constant habit.

But I wanted to meet him, I was really into him. I thought maybe he was actually busy, but then there are many guys who are 100 times more busy than him but always have time for their better half. Why couldn't he take out time for me? I thought maybe he was dating someone whom he broke up with and that's why he proposed me. I was making a lot of assumptions. I even thought that he might be staying with somebody so he had to stop talking to me when he was with her. Because usually these things only happen.

I wanted to trust him, I wanted him to love me back like I did. I wanted to tell him I love him.

He came and texted me "I am here for you baby."

I was really excited to see him. I didn't go to pick him up from the airport but he came straight from there to our favourite 5-star hotel's restaurant, we had lunch together. It was a very long flight so I suggested he should rest.

But he told me "I didn't want to inform my family that I am here but I had to"

"Oh"

"I am leaving for home tonight, I will come back after 2 days."

His house was 4 hours away from the city. He said he would come back after 2 days which meant we had just 2 days to spend together.

He didn't call me when he went home, not even a single message. When it was the time to meet, he called and we decided upon the same restaurant again.

"Aditi how are you feeling?"

"I don't think it's going to work out between us Arjun"

"You don't have time, I really don't like repeating the same thing again and again but I want somebody who gives me time. I don't like your disappearing for days just like that."

"But there's always something genuine Aditi."

"Hmm"

"Please don't say no like that."

"I am sorry Arjun."

I came back home. I wanted him to know that it can't go on. When he was out it was like that, when he came here, again it was the same.

He kept calling but I didn't feel like receiving.

"Give me a chance Aditi."

"I am observing this past many months Arjun."

"Last chance, it's my last day here tomorrow please."

"Ok"

1.5

I wanted to see whether it worked out or not. There were several better options waiting for me. But I liked his company and I really liked his words. He could keep up the conversation alive. That is why I kept accepting his unbelievable excuses and always took him back.

Beauty fades with time, but when we are older, it's the conversations that make us keep falling in love with that person. He was really good with words.

We met again, this time at a mall. We decided to spend the entire day together, starting from breakfast until dinner.

After lunch, he said he will shop for his sisters. We did a lot of shopping for them. Even I paid for a few things I liked to gift them.

I thought maybe he will buy something for me also but he didn't. He didn't get anything from Ireland when he came here. In fact he asked me if there was anything if I wanted to gift his mother. I felt ridiculous at that time. Usually with everyone, guys pamper girls with presents but here the scene was just the opposite.

It was dinner time, he was shopping for himself and there were two guys staring at me, Arjun noticed them. It was like he enjoyed when men looked at me and I hated it. I wanted my boyfriend to be protective about me and break the bones of anyone who even gave me a second glance but Arjun was being really creepy.

This day changed my perception about him. All the liking, attraction, respect for him had gone down the drain.

We bid each other goodbye. He left for Ireland that night. He was undoubtedly very stingy-not for himself but for his girl.

He spent a lot on his family, himself, his friends, but not on his girlfriend. My friend who introduced me to him had told me his ex left him because he forgot her birthday gift. No. The scene would have been like, she would have watched him shopping for himself throughout the year along with her, but would have never offered anything. In fact, he would have been asking her to buy him stuff-like he did with me. And when her birthday came, she must definetely be expecting something. But to her surprise, he got nothing.

I got a clear picture about this and I was literally imagining this. I found it really dumb of her to leave him for such a reason, but anyone else or I who would be dealing with a guy like him would do the same.

After reaching Ireland, he didn't call me for 10 days. Again the same old drama, I was sick and tired of the gaps he gave me and I had explained to him several times it won't work out if he kept doing it.

When he started calling, I didn't respond to his calls for a month. After that, he started calling more frantically and got in touch with my friends to connect with me. I received his call.

"Where have you been Aditi, are you crazy?"

"Crazy like you."

"Tell me where were you. I am sure you are seeing some guy."

"No"

"Don't lie."

"Do you do what you just accused me of?"

He was silent.

"No Aditi, I was worried about you."

"I was giving you a taste of your own medicine"

"And the medicine is very bitter", he laughed.

"How are you?"

"Bad. Without you I am bad", he replied.

After that day. He didn't miss a day without calling me. His habit of disappearing had diminished.

1.6

We spoke endlessly everytime. We never lost interest in each other and never run out of topics to discuss. I knew he was stingy but I overlooked it. Not everyone is perfect.

I fell in love with him more and more every day and he told me the same. It was not hard staying away as it didn't feel like a long distance relationship. Although there was a huge distance barrier but we were always connected.

He made me feel that his entire life revolved around me. He asked me everything-like what he should wear today, what he should eat, where he should shop from, what exercise to do at the gym, which vegetable to buy.

Now, who wouldn't like anything of that sort. I always wanted somebody like him. He had changed for the better. In the previous months, he would avoid me for days. It was nothing like this now.

On my birthday he didn't gift me anything. Our friends knew we were dating, they knew his nature, they knew he was stingy. One of them told me to send him the link of a present I wanted from him and see whether he would send it. We were sitting there determining the level of his stinginess. They told me if he would continue to behave like this it would be very difficult to live with him, he would fail to fulfill his basic duties as a husband also, forget financing his wife. Their words somehow seemed reasonable to me.

I did exactly what they suggested.

"Arjun I want these earrings"

"Ok dear."

I was so happy. It would be the first gift in one year.

The next day he told me "My credit card is not working."

I understood this disease of being stingy is incurable.

"It's ok."

"I am using cash here, once my card starts working I will send it to you"

"Ok"

I remember he had 7 credit cards and he gets a huge salary that most Indian engineers crave for.

Soon he conveniently forgot about the present, I also didn't remind him.

After a few days, he sent me pictures of things he was buying to send home for his friends and he kept asking me what to buy or what not to buy for them. Those earrings were the first thing I asked him for which did not strike his mind while he was shopping for more expensive stuff for his friends back in India.

I didn't say anything neither did I give him any hint.

I loved him, his companionship mattered to me. But I was wondering if he couldn't take care of my happiness by fulfilling small wishes, what would he do later.

I was financially independent, I had enough money of my own. He belonged to a poor family, he struggled hard, became highly qualified and acquired a good job. I belonged to a highly aristocratic family, always led a lavish life, was working in one of the best companies in Gurgaon. I didn't need his presents, neither was I greedy for it, but a little effort sometimes is highly appreciated.

1.7

I was at a nightclub with my friends when a guy who looked very familiar came near me and said "Hi"

"Hello"

"You are Aditi right?"

"Yes, I am sorry I am not being able to recognize you."

"I am Akhil, Arjun's friend."

"Okay, that is why your face looks familiar."

"Must have seen me in photographs with him."

"Yes", I agreed.

"Look Aditi, there is something that I would like to tell you."

"Yes?"

"I don't know how to place this, I shouldn't be saying this to you also as Arjun is my friend."

"You can tell me", I was getting curious.

"Look", he pulled out his phone from his pocket.

He was browsing through his gallery and stopped at a picture.

"Here it is", he pointed.

I saw the picture and said, "Who are they?"

Okay, so this is how it was. Two men were kissing each other ON THE LIPS, one was holding the other behind his neck passionately, the other guy had his eyes closed and it seemed both were having an erotic time together.

"Look properly", he said.

"What is there to look Akhil?"

"You still couldn't relate?" he asked impatiently.

I zoomed into the picture and to my surprise, the guy with his eyes opened and the one who appeared to take the initiative of kissing was nobody else but Arjun. I was shocked, the phone slipped from my hand.

Akhil understood I have figured out it's Arjun.

"Can you send me the picture?"

"Only if you promise not to reveal that I gave it to you"

"Who has this picture apart from you?" I asked dubiously.

"Our entire friend circle Aditi."

"Is he gay?"

"You think you have to ask me this?"

"No, I mean it could be a prank too?", I asked uncertainly, hoping it was a prank.

"No"

I was silent.

"He is a bi-sexual, but he has very less inclination towards women."

"Can you explain?"

"He is more happy with men, rather than women. He can do it with both but he prefers men." he added

I felt sick. I seriously felt sick.

"I am informing this to you now as he did the same with my girlfriend which led to our break up, he has done it with many other guys too. Inspite of sitting in Ireland, he is not letting us stay at peace."

"You too?"

"I was"

"Now what does that mean?"

"I am no longer into men Aditi."

"Why is he wanting to marry me then?"

"He had better job offers in Delhi but he denied, he wanted to stay far away from Indian culture, primarily from his orthodox family. They would disown him if they found out he was sleeping with men"

"But that is not the answer to my question Akhil."

"He is getting married only for the sake of his parents. They are pressurizing him to get married as soon as possible. He has already crossed 35 years."

"Why didn't he tell me?"

"Because you would leave him."

"I don't disrespect bisexuals, everyone has the right to do whatever they please, they all have their own preferences and interests. These things are very common now a days, my best friend is gay, I really don't care. But I didn't want to marry somebody like that."

"Many women are not open to this", he said.

"What should I do now?"

"Up to you."

"How should I question him?"

"Don't."

"Then?"

"As if he is going to accept it."

"Why won't he?", I asked.

"Just leave him like that because even after marrying you he won't stay with you. I know Arjun too well"

"Why?", my mind was bursting with innumerable questions.

"He has plans of keeping his wife with his parents at the village, he will tell you he will take you to Ireland along with him but he will not. He might take you there for a few days and send you back to Gurgaon or to his parents."

"He didn't say anything like that."

"Why would he Aditi?"

I couldn't handle all this anymore. I just went back home and slept.

1.8

Arjun didn't call me. His gaps started again. Where the hell did he go when he was not speaking to me. But I was madly in love with him. I always wanted him to be around me.

4 - 5 days passed but no calls, I called him but he gave quick replies, each conversation lasted no more than 5 minutes.

I went to the gym and spoke to my best friend about it. I didn't tell her it's Arjun otherwise she would have made fun of me.

Nobody could make out it's Arjun in the picture, unless and until someone hovers above your head like Akhil did and make you think like you are solving a brain teaser.

Arjun looked maximum 25 in the picture, that was around 10 years back.

I showed her the picture.

"Why are you showing me gay romance Aditi?"

"Nazia do you think it can be a prank or something?"

"Why are you concerned and who are they?"

I was just wanting to hear from her that it could be a prank. I just didn't want to believe in what Akhil said. I didn't want to leave Arjun.

"No way, Are you blind? They are holding each other like couples do."

I had nothing to say.

I went back home and called Arjun, I wanted to ask him about this. He was too busy to even answer my call but he texted back-

In a meeting love, I am sorry for being the worst boyfriend in this world for not giving you time. But always remember, not even a single moment passes without thinking of you Aditi. I am going to call you at night.

He didn't. I waited the entire day and night, missed office the next day, still waiting for his call but he didn't.

He called after 2 days again with so many excuses. I asked him to check his mail while I spoke to him and asked him to open it while speaking to me.

He laughed and said, "Baby I was high, we were drunk, it is a very old picture which you can easily make out, we didn't know what we were doing."

"Are you bisexual?"

He started laughing his ass off and said, "Not at all my little baby, I won't even ask you who has sent you the picture because my friends were also there who clicked this."

"I am straight, I only love women and most importantly that woman is you Aditi."

"I thought you were gay or something."

He laughed again.

I was so relieved, I was not being able to cope up with the thoughts that were going on in my mind. I only saw these things on television or internet and it was going to be a part of my life, the guy I was madly in love with was on the verges of being labelled as bisexual. I couldn't believe these things happen so openly here and Arjun couldn't be that. He was way too charismatic to be tagged as that. This happening in real life seemed impossible, I never knew these things existed. Even if my bestie was gay, it was just evident from the way he walked, spoke, laughed. Arjun didn't show any of these signs, not even once.

1.9

My friends always told me Arjun didn't deserve me as he never gave me the attention I deserved. Communication was very little from his side, there were those gaps I always hated but whenever he called he would make me feel as if I am the only girl he was talking to, he gave me all updates of each day we didn't speak. But nothing should have kept him apart from calling, at least once. What could keep him so busy? It was not the first time that he was staying alone, he had been out of India over 8 years.

Everything was just perfect about him except that he would simply disappear for days without any clue of where he is and what he is up to.

Whenever I felt like giving up hope on him, he gave me reasons to stay.

Everything was going perfectly normal, he was calling regularly, we spoke everyday. I knew he didn't love me as much as I loved him.

He could do without speaking to me for days, for me one day without him was struggle. I liked his company, I enjoyed every word he said, I loved the way he said my name. We were around 8000 kilometers away from each other, every day was difficult without him. But distance means so little, when someone special means so much.

I never forced him to talk to me, never clinged upon him, was never pushy-I wanted to be all of it, but I didn't. I was practicing extreme self control with him.

We looked like a cute couple, he was not very tall, in fact just an inch taller than me. He didn't mind looking short whenever I wore heels. He was fair, average built but had a good personality. There were already better looking guys after me but my heart was stuck with him. I was so jealous of people who could be around him everyday. I wished I could be with him forever. Distance gives us a reason to miss and love harder. No matter how far apart we were, he was always on my mind.

He called one evening and said, "Aditi, lets end this relationship."

Both of us were silent for a moment.

He broke the silence by his naughty laughter and added, "Let's end this long distance relationship baby."

"Are you coming?"

"Forever", he said.

I couldn't control my happiness.

"I am coming to stay with you here, then I will take you back to Ireland with me."

1.10

Whenever I was going away from him, he did something that immediately pulled me back to him. I was so excited that we were going to be together. He said he was coming but he didn't say when.

The next evening while I was at office, I received a text from him which read –

"Sorry baby, I can't come. I think I can't keep up to your expectations. We need to break up."

I didn't reply anything, neither did I call him, nor did I seek any explanation, to hell with that moron.

When it was time for me to leave, again I received a text from him –

"I am sorry Aditi, I shouldn't have done this."

When I was standing at my office gate thinking what he had done, he texted-

"Look straight."

What the hell did I just see? I was rubbing my eyes as I couldn't believe it was him standing right in front of me.

I ran towards him and hugged him, "Why so much drama Arjun? You made me cry"

"Awww my little baby is crying", he said while he was wiping my tears.

"I love you Arjun."

"I love you more Aditi."

We went to a coffee shop nearby and just looked at each other for more than half an hour, without saying a single word.

Now this man really knew how to make me happy. I was so dumb to think of him like that. I couldn't stay without him.

"Aditi I am going home tonight, I will come back after the weekend, that is on Monday."

"hmm", I said sadly.

Why did he have to always go back home, why couldn't he stay with me for a few days and then go back. I wanted to be with him.

On Sunday he called me and said, "I am going to Bangalore for 3 days tomorrow, my friends want to catch up, I will come to you straight from the airport."

Again he went. Why wasn't he desiring me as much as I was desiring him. I was getting more upset. He was in India, he could have stayed a little longer with me, why was he doing this everytime.

In Bangalore, we spoke normally, regular phone calls and texts. It was the time for him to come back. From the airport he called and said, "Baby I need to go back home, I will come back day after tomorrow to see you I promise, I love you and I am sorry, don't get mad at me."

I was already mad at him, I wanted to kill him for this. Why he left me hanging like this? He makes me feel so wanted and every time he fails to turn up whenever we are supposed to meet.

1.11

I didn't receive his calls as I was pissed off with him. He kept on calling every ten minutes. He had sent over a thousand texts.

His sister called me and said, "Aditi are you upset with Arjun?"

"He made you call me right?"

"No. No. I wanted to speak to you". I could hear him laughing from behind.

"Please speak to him, he is getting very worried."

Arjun took the phone from his sister and said, "Baby I have come here only for you, don't get angry."

"Yeah! probably that's why it's been over a week since you have come to India and you could take out just an hour for me."

"I am sorry love, I will see you tomorrow."

"Your tomorrow never comes."

"It will. I love you."

I disconnected the phone and slept. The next morning I woke and saw heavy rainfall and flood. It was the first time in many years that the rain was at this pace. His house was a four-hour drive from mine, but he stayed in his friend's flat whenever he came to Gurgaon. Arjun drove in such a risky weather and was right on time the next day to see me.

I was not allowed to leave my house, there was high alert in the news regarding this rain, many people died on the road due to lightning and tree fall.

Arjun called and said, "Love, I am waiting for you, Will you please come?"

I said, "I really want to, but it's raining heavily."

"I will wait for you until you come and I am not going to leave from here."

He waited 7 hours in the mall for me and when I ultimately sneeked out of my house I was able to meet him.

But I saw him with his friend Arif. Arjun said he called Arif as he was getting bored and he wanted some company, so in between, they watched a movie together, did some shopping and had lunch.

I thought it was fair enough.

Arjun told me, "Arif will leave after sometime, let's order dinner Aditi, he will have the starter and mocktail, then leave"

"I want privacy with you Arjun. I need space to talk to you."

"I understand baby but it would be very rude of us to just ask him to leave like that."

I agreed.

We finished the main course, ordered the dessert but Arif was just not leaving and I was losing my cool. Arjun seemed just okay about it.

I had come for a very limited time, Arjun knew, but he was just not finding out time for me.

Ultimately, I just excused myself for the washroom and called Arjun, "You shouldn't have come only, go back to Ireland" and disconnected the line.

When I came back to my seat, Arjun gave Arif that look which was obvious that he should leave.

Arif said, "You are very beautiful Aditi, Arjun is really lucky. I am leaving now and it was nice meeting you."

I smiled back and just said thanks.

Arjun said, "My goodness, you really get angry."

"You are the reason behind it"

Again I saw Arif coming up to the table out of nowhere, I seriously felt like smacking him on the face this time. Not only him but Arjun also.

"Arjun you left Aditi's gift in my car."

"Thanks Arif" he again gestured at him and asked him to leave.

Arjun handed me the presents, it was wrapped beautifully. Now this was the best part, first present from him and I was really not expecting it. I had actually given up on him thinking he is super duper stingy.

I opened the present and there was a nice purse from Burberry and a box of premium chocolates.

I was really happy, I already had a large collection of Burberry bags.

"Thanks Arjun!" I said while I hugged him.

Soon we left and he promised to meet every day for the next 5 days.

1.12

"I am waiting for you Arjun, where are you?"

"I am stuck with some work baby, it will take me an hour more."

"I will wait for you, come soon."

It was over an hour, I was still waiting for him, he turned up after 3 hours. I was all alone at the mall, waiting for him, he didn't give me any specific time so I could go back home or call somebody to give me company till he came.

"I am so sorry Aditi, I made you wait."

We had shisha and pasta and left.

The next day again he made me wait for 2 hours.

I was really upset with this, nobody ever made me wait before, I didn't mind waiting for him also, but he said something really stupid once he came "Tired of waiting?"

"Somewhat", I said in a sleepy voice

"It was difficult waiting that day for you Aditi."

"You took revenge?"

"Hahahaha. No baby."

"You just said that Arjun."

"Just kidding love."

"Hmm"

"Let's go for a movie today."

"Okay but I have to leave at 7."

"We will watch half of it then."

"What's the point?"

"Just like that."

"Stupid."

"We can watch the remaining half tomorrow."

When I reached home his words were still ringing on my head. He was actually making me wait because I made him wait.

We went for paintball the next day, he was an hour late.

He knew I had a time to maintain to go back home, I missed my office every day just to meet him, he should have respected that. He made me feel as if he was doing a favour meeting me. When he knew I am coming for 4 hours. He would come 2 hours late so we were able to spend just the half time together. He always did that.

The same thing happened for the rest of the days we intended to meet.

I was not feeling good.

I told him, "Arjun I have fever I will not be able to meet you today."

"Aditi till when will you recover?"

"How can I say that?"

"Maybe 3 days?"

"How will I know when my fever will subside?"

"Baby you rest, I will go to Lucknow to meet my school friends and come back tomorrow."

He was strange. Everyday he told me how special I was to him and we were spending this beautiful time on our courtship. He wanted to get married as soon as possible. Everyone was happy with me at his place, nobody knew about him at mine. But I could easily convince my family and there was nothing inconvincible about Arjun. I didn't like the fact that I told him I was having fever, while I was not, just to see his reaction and what did he do? So easily and swiftly he chalked out his plans. It didn't matter to him much. I didn't matter to him.

I didn't stop him this time, I just wanted to stop telling him what to do or what not to do. I always told him I didn't like the gaps he gave me while he was in Ireland but he didn't change. Now that he was in India, he should have spent maximum time with me but he was planning his outings with friends I never knew existed. I was understanding his priorities pretty well.

We didn't speak much when he was in Lucknow. I didn't call him once, I just wanted to see how much effort is he actually taking into our relationship.

While he was in Lucknow, he said, "Can I ask you for a gift?"

"Sure"

"I want an iPad Aditi."

"Which one?"

"The best one."

The one he wanted was around sixty thousand rupees, half of my one month's salary. I told him I will gift it to him after a month.

When he came back, he wanted to meet me so we met.

He was behaving a little strangely, as if he wanted love. I had never seen him like this before, he looked a little disturbed, I tried asking him but he didn't respond, he was very secretive, he never told me much about what was going on in his mind.

"Can't you gift me an iPad now?" He asked suddenly.

"Why can't you buy it yourself?"

"I can, but I want it from you Aditi."

"This is not cheap Arjun, it is costly, I asked for a month's time. My parents have money that doesn't mean I ask them for it. I earn and I pay for my expenses."

"Ya fine", he replied with a disgusted face.

Why did he have a disgusted face. Firstly he was so stingy himself, then he asked for my new phone worth eighty thousand before he went to Lucknow to show off to his friends but I denied, then he was asking for an expensive present. What the hell was wrong with him?

1.13

We were clicking pictures from his phone and I was swiping through our selfies. I saw Arif's picture, the next one was Arif with a baby.

I asked Arjun, "You didn't tell me Arif was married."

"I forgot"

"You told me he is in a live-in relationship with his girlfriend."

"Yeah"

"I am not understanding Arjun."

"Why do you need to understand?"

"Why can't you?"

"Aditi he married somebody his parents selected for him but she is a villager, he has a baby from her but he doesn't like her so he is staying with somebody else in the city."

I didn't want to comment on anything.

Arjun wanted to use my phone to call Arif as his phone's battery was almost 0. He excused himself and went to the side to speak to him.

When I returned home, I checked the automatic call recorder app on my phone and listened to their conversation's recording as I was getting curious about what they were really up to.

Everything was perfectly fine in their talk, until it reached the end in which Arif said, "Miss you darling."

Arjun replied, "Will see you tonight handsome."

I kept the phone aside. I was getting nervous. Whatever Akhil had told me was right. But I thought could it be a "bro code"?

Many girls also call each other sweetie, sweetheart, that doesn't mean they are lesbians.

We met again but this time my curiosity was at its peak. This time I asked for his phone to make a call, went to the ladies washroom while pretending to speak, checked his gallery and went through the pictures.

I was disgusted with what I saw, Arjun was getting intimate with few guys and the location in his phone of those pictures showed Lucknow, then there was Arif and his girlfriend kissing, Arif and Arjun kissing, Arjun and Arif's girlfriend kissing.

I went through older pictures, Arjun making out with two guys at the same time, location was Ireland.

I immediately transferred these pictures to my phone, then I went through his messages and the first one was from Arif which read - "You had fun with Mary, now it's time for Aditi."

Arjun's reply - "I am trying."

Arif – "How long dude?"

Arjun – "I will get married to her first, or else she will slip out of my hand like Veena."

I was disgusted. I took snaps of these messages as well, called somebody random to just show the duration in call log of his phone. I returned the phone to him and said I wasn't feeling well.

1.14

After coming back home, I started crying. I cried all night. Arjun's plans with me were so dirty. I never imagined he could do such a thing. Akhil warned me of this. Arjun was wife swapping, it's disgusting. I hated him for this. His intentions were so filthy.

Arjun called and texted me several times but I didn't respond, I just kept my phone on silent mode and far away from me.

He was bisexual, he wanted his wife to sleep with his friend.

He used to give me gaps while he was in Ireland because he was having fun with his partners there. He ignored me here and it was all because he lacked interest in women and he was more inclined towards men.

I met him after a week for the last time, I told him I had fever. He understood something was wrong as I never ignored him no matter how sick I was. He tried to come close to me for the first time as he thought I was in double mind to leave him, I pushed him away.

I didn't tell him I have come to know the truth, I didn't have the courage to repeat these things with him. I loved him with all my heart but he broke it. He was fooling me.

I got the present along which he got for me and gave it back to him.

He was surprised, he didn't think anything like that could happen.

"I am sorry Arjun, I can't get married to you."

"What? Why?"

I lied to him and said, "My uncle won't allow."

"Now what does your uncle have to do with us Aditi?"

"He is the head of our family and we act upon his decisions."

"I will make them understand", he said.

"Nothing will change his decision Arjun."

He held my hand and tried to calm me down, he was exchanging those "full of love" looks we used to give each other when we just started dating.

I didn't want to tell him I know the truth, I didn't want to complicate things further.

I left from there.

He called me every day, I didn't respond.

One day he texted - Aditi I am going back to Ireland, meet me for the last time.

I didn't reply.

Again a text from him came – I will wait for you tomorrow between 12 pm-4 pm where we last met. Hope to see you. Don't want your reply. I will still wait.

I didn't want to go, but I wanted to see him, I truely loved him. I reached there around 4 pm but didn't meet him, was just observing him from a distance. He must have assumed that I am not going to come and neither did he see me.

Arif walked in with his girlfriend around 4.30 pm, both put hands across her waist, this was the cheapest incident I had witnessed in my life. I felt like puking.

Arjun was going to give me this life. This would have been my future with Arjun. I met Akhil coincidentally there, he saw me spying at them but didn't say anything. He just smiled and went away.

Akhil proposed me after few days and I said yes. Soon we left for our job together in California and decided to get married there.

2. FAIZ & MAIRA

2.1

A new friend request from Faiz. The notification blinked on my phone. Within 2-3 minutes, another notification appeared on another site I was a member at. Within seconds his message came and our chat went like -

"Hi Maira."

"Hi"

"This is Faiz, I am 27 and I have my own business, I really like your profile."

"Ok"

"You are really pretty, I wonder whether you are an angel or human?"

I wanted to write- Awwww.. that's so sweet of you, thank you. But, I choose to write "Thanks". I wanted to be formal.

"I know it's a little strange but I am proposing you for marriage straight away. Actually, I have seen you a couple of times coincidentally and when I saw your profile, I couldn't resist talking to you. I always wanted to come and speak to you but couldn't. I am sure you must have never noticed me earlier."

"Oh... I didn't notice you", I just said this.

We started chatting online and gradually started knowing each other. He seemed to be a nice, decent guy who used to flirt at times. He just couldn't stop praising about my beauty every time.

He wanted my number, he was pretty serious about me. I asked him to speak to my father first, if he agreed then we could proceed. They spoke for half an hour over the phone, it was like a rigorous interview. He was rejected by dad for reasons unknown. I didn't bother to ask as Faiz hardly mattered to me. For 3 days he didn't text me, suddenly one day I received his call. He acquired my number from some mutual friend.

"Can we talk as friends?"

"What's the point?", I asked hesitantly.

"No harm in talking", he insisted.

I agreed.

We spoke very often. He was the one to take most of the initiative.

I would reply to him sometimes, most of the time the ratio of his to my messages was 10: 1. But he kept on trying to keep up the conversation. He would always praise me that made me really happy otherwise there was nothing to feel so great about him. He was just average, or probably below average in looks. His conversations were also boring.

"Let's meet", he said.

"I don't think it would be right."

"Why do you think so much Maira?"

"I don't think I will be comfortable Faiz."

"Give me a chance."

"Ok but just for half an hour."

"As you say but you will not want to leave, I can bet you on that." said Faiz.

2.2

We were about to meet but the same day there was an earthquake. I had come from the parlour all prepared that day to meet him but we had to call off the plan.

We decided to meet after a few days. He was waiting for me at my favourite restaurant. I saw a glimpse of him and turned back, there was an instinct from within which repeatedly said – it's not going to work out.

He started calling, I received.

"Where are you?"

"Right here", I said while walking in the restaurant.

He stood up to greet me and then we ordered.

I didn't like his company much but it felt just okay. We were there for an hour and when I was about to leave he said, "You are beautiful, I wish we could marry soon."

I felt little awkward-why did he say that so abruptly.

We spoke on phone several times, started meeting once a week. On my birthday he got me a beautiful watch and a ring and proposed me again. I didn't accept the ring. I actually said a "no" straight away.

He said, "Take as much time you want, I will always wait for your answer."

We kept on meeting, sometimes at my favorite restaurant, sometimes his. He always wanted to make me feel wanted. He agreed with whatever I said and respected every decision of mine. One day I said yes.

He kept me happy, I didn't meet him much. He would work in his office and I would study in college. We had our routine sorted, we would check upon each other throughout the day but mostly speak over the phone at night.

3

I liked him because he was hardworking and independent. He was the man of his house, he lived with his parents. Most of the decisions would be his at his place. He had an elder sister and an elder brother. Both lived in separate cities and visited each year for 2 months.

He didn't have many friends, very few, in fact I used to push him to catch up with his friends when I went out with mine. It was nice being with him but there was not much happiness from within. It felt like our relationship lacked something.

Soon he wanted to meet my parents, it was already October so we decided upon December. We were leaving from a coffee shop at a mall, that's when I met my school friend Nima.

"He stays at my building, Maira. I know him" she whispered in my ears.

Faiz didn't like the fact that we knew each other. He asked me to stay away from her as he felt she was a little weird.

Faiz and I met a couple of times after that, I caught him staring at a girl and he knew I caught him eyeing her.

"Why are you even looking at her?"

"I have a habit of looking."

"What?", I couldn't believe what he just said.

"I have a habit of observing people I mean to say."

"But I don't like this habit of yours."

"It can't change Maira."

I hated him for this.

"Get lost", I told him and left. I didn't receive his calls for 2 days. But then he was really sorry so we patched up.

He went out of the city for some work. The same day I had an invitation in Nima's place for lunch. She told me many things about Faiz and when I was about to leave she said, "I hope you know about Tania."

"Tania?"

"What? Seriously you don't know Maira?"

"No, tell me."

"Faiz should have told you about her."

Her flat's door was opened so we could see the elevator as we spoke. Suddenly she held my hand and pointed toward's the elevator and said, "She is Tania".

"Okay, But what is the matter between them?"

"Both were dating each other for the past 4 years. She broke up with him just a month before Faiz proposed to you. Since their break up Faiz had been following her everywhere to get her back. Instead, she complained to his parents. Her parents spoke to everyone in the complex, a meeting was held and Faiz was strictly asked not to bother her anymore so he stopped it."

"Does she stay here?", I asked.

"Just the opposite flat of his."

"I didn't know that Nima."

"Anyways she is nothing in front of you, be it beauty or qualification. She's a dumbass and right now she is dating another guy in her office."

It was such a coincidence that I could see Tania the same time Nima spoke about her. Maybe Faiz still had feelings for her. Probably that's why he asked me to stay away from Nima as he didn't want me to know about this affair of his which I obviously wouldn't be comfortable with.

Past is past, I agree but his past was just living next door.

He called me several times that day but I didn't receive. Ultimately I confronted him about Tania and he acted as if she didn't exist.

"Who Tania?"

"Don't act smart Faiz."

"Nima told you right?"

"Why didn't you tell me?"

"I am sorry. I don't love her anymore. I have already found compassion in you baby. You are my life now"

I didn't accept it. I spoke to Tania directly. Nima gave me her number.

"Hi Tania."

"Hi."

"I wanted to know whether there is something between you and Faiz now."

"No. It's over, I am getting engaged to my colleague next month."

I was satisfied with her answer, she also made it clear they didn't matter to each other anymore but I still didn't start speaking to Faiz.

2.3

The next morning I saw hundreds of missed calls from his mom and dad when I woke up. I had never spoken to them before. I received her call and she said :

"Maira, Faiz is really upset, please speak to him."

"Ok."

"There is nothing between Tania and him. Trust me." she passed on the phone to his father who repeated the same.

Faiz thought I broke up with him, I actually had. But I decided to stay after Tania said she didn't want him .I spoke to Faiz that night. He did a video call and showed me his teary eyes which seemed so red. It was sure he cried all day. We met and he really felt sorry. I had never seen him like that. He said he loved me and made me feel special in every way possible. I started to love him even more than before. Our love had become more intense and we started meeting more often.

The date for him to meet my parents was very close. In spite of dad rejecting him, I knew he would agree if I asked him to. I was happy we were going to be together for the rest of our lives.

He spoke to me about many things. He shared everything with me. He even spoke about his 3-4 other exes he didn't mention earlier - in case I found out again. But what made me sad was about his sister Nur.

"Nur's in laws had done black magic on her right after her marriage, she lost 7 babies in miscarriage. The last miscarriage was when they were on their way to the hospital for delivery. Once her mother in law died, she had a baby girl. The next year again she had a boy. She was able to give birth to two children after the death of her mother in law, even her husband agreed to it." Faiz said these with tears rolling down his cheeks.

"My mom will love you a lot", he added. "She loves my sister in law. In fact, she is very fond of her. You will really enjoy here."

Everything was perfect for us. But suddenly his calls reduced, earlier we would speak all night but suddenly he stopped calling saying his brother had come and he was sharing his room as the other room's air conditioner was not working.

I thought it might be true. But this went on for two weeks. In these 2 weeks, his calls hardly came at night, he would call during the day though. I started feeling annoyed. I wanted to speak to him. I was missing him.

2.4

It was just five days before he would meet my parents and we were supposed to meet that day.

I called him. He didn't receive. He just sent a text which read – Not well, food poisoning, will call after I wake up.

We didn't speak the entire day. The next morning again I called him. His staff received and said, "Sir is not here."

Then where the hell was he? Did he die that he couldn't talk? I was really mad at him.

Nima called me and started consoling me. She said, "let's go out, you will feel better."

"Feel better? Why? What happened?"

"Don't you know about Faiz?"

My heart skipped a beat. I thought something really bad happened to him. I cursed myself for thinking ill of him. As it is he had problem at work, then his brother shared his room and now food poisoning.

"Hello?" she said as I was silently busy thinking about him.

"Yes, tell me Nima?"

"You know they are getting married right?"

"Who they?"

"Faiz and Tania."

"Whatttt?" I couldn't speak. I was shocked.

"Three days back she cut her wrist for Faiz as she was getting insecure that he was with you", she said.

"Then?", I mustered courage and spoke as normally as I could without breaking down in front of her.

"He made her jealous, he kept sending her your and his pictures throughout so she could come running back to him."

"Oh.. then..", I asked.

"Since then he is in hospital with her and they are getting married next week."

"Ok..."

"He is such a loser, he didn't have the capacity to get her back on his own so he used you to get her do this. He is such a jerk. Bloody creep."

I disconnected the line and texted him – All the best for your new life.

Immediately after that he called and acted normal as if nothing happened. I again confronted him about Tania. He didn't accept it.

"She attempted suicide for you."

"No"

"Don't lie again."

"I am not."

He again made me speak to his mother who denied this. Faiz said he wanted to meet me but I said no. He wanted to meet me along with his brother.

His brother called me and said, "Maira, he loves you, don't worry"

Nima made me speak to Tania's sister who was also in the hospital. She did a video call and showed me Tania's condition, her wrist cut with Faiz sitting next to her. He didn't know the video call was on.

Faiz had already done nikah with her in the hospital that day but he kept calling me to say it wasn't true. I knew he and his family were lying. I stopped all contact with him.

He played with me, he used me to get her back, he broke my heart, he betrayed me. I couldn't believe all this. Too much had happened to me that day, I couldn't gather myself.

2.5

I was devastated. That night again there was an earthquake. Like the first day, we were about to meet. It is said when God is angry he inflicts his people with disasters like earthquakes.

I was browsing through our pictures and deleting them one by one. I cried a lot that day. It was like a part of me had died. The child within me died. My heart was stabbed a million times by the man I was going to spend my life with.

I soon saw Faiz and Tania's wedding picture. I wiped my tears. My friends fixed many dates for me, I didn't deny. I was so frustrated by what he had done to me I started dating many men, one by one in order to forget him but couldn't. I was very simple, always stayed away from modeling but my friend suggested and it actually worked. I got many offers and I became a famous face in the city in a very short time. I transformed from a very simple young girl to a glamorous woman. From a no-experience baby to a mature independent kickass woman.

Within 5 months I heard they had a baby girl which meant that they made out while Faiz was meeting me and wanting to marry me. I calculated the months along with Nima. The month of conception was Tania's birthday and their child was born in his birthday month.

I started hating Faiz more. I thought maybe he loved me – at least for that time he was with me. But in real, he was sleeping with her while dating me.

After 2 years, I met Zaid, a very handsome guy my friend introduced me to. He looked so handsome, all girls would stare at him, but he wouldn't stare at anyone. He would just look at me. His eyes were only for me & only at me. This is what I always wanted.

He proposed me. I immediately said yes. We decided to get married after one year.

We were just leaving a mall when Faiz saw me with him. I completely avoided Faiz and made my face as if I had seen a piece of shit.

Zaid knew about him so it didn't matter to him or me.

The same night, I received a call from an unknown number.

"Hi", said the person.

I knew it was Faiz.

"Who is this?" I still asked.

"Maira, I am sorry. It's me Faiz."

I disconnected the line.

Again he called and said, "I am sorry, I really am. I know whatever I did is beyond forgiveness but I need you back in my life. Tania left me for the guy she was dating at her workplace. She left our baby girl with me. Please marry me. I know you are getting married to Zaid but please don't do that."

I said, "This is not possible. I am not like you. It's not a game. I don't play with others like you."

I disconnected the line again. I immediately called Zaid and told him about this. I was not feeling comfortable anymore. As it is Zaid wanted to marry me as soon as possible, I only wanted a year's time.

"Let's get married", Zaid told me again.

"Let's do it baby."

"I am making all the preparations,you just get ready and come to the venue tomorrow. I am sending the dress, jewellery and makeup artist to your place."

I felt like the happiest woman on this planet when he told me this. Our parents were also happy with our decision.

We got married.

Nima came to our wedding, clicked pictures and sent it to Faiz without my knowledge.

I received a message from him – Congrats. So this was your answer to my appeal. Anyways all the best.

I replied with a screenshot of my message wishing him all the best for his new life which I sent to him 2 years back when he left me.

People who hurt us, eventually face their own karma. Time heals all wounds, sitting back and watching karma take your revenge is an amazing feeling.

3. SAIF & ZARA

3.1

I was enjoying my life to the fullest. I had everything in life anyone could possibly wish for. Amazing group of friends, best of branded clothes, jewelleries, outings to the most happening places in town.In spite of this, I felt something missing. All these just could not fill up the emptiness of not having a partner.

It was a regular day for me. I went to my university then gym and finally to a departmental store where it took really long to complete the billing. Something was wrong with the system. Just behind me stood a guy, bossing around the store.

I thought maybe he owns it or something. But he did not. I was too irritated with the cashier to even give him another glance. But I could feel his gaze on me.

I completed the billing and as I was about to leave the store, I saw him holding the door for me. He did not buy what he had in his shopping cart as he did not want to miss the opportunity to talk. I did not want to talk to him at all. But the way he began the conversation I just couldn't resist listening to Saif.

It was the first time in my life that I actually entertained a stranger and yes we exchanged numbers on spot. I checked my phone once I returned home & saw texts sent by Saif. I found it really strange but it was not like I didn't want to reply. I started replying and then we started speaking on phone. I just took him as a friend, nothing more than that.

3.2

We met the next day at a restaurant, which I generally avoid at the mall due to the excessive crowd. I told him I want to go somewhere else but he insisted on that restaurant. He suddenly started speaking about his past relationship. I never asked him this but he started off on his own.

He said, "I got engaged to a girl called Uma who used me for money. One day I played a prank with her by saying I have become bankrupt so she dumped me after hearing this within 48 hours."

I could see his face becoming red with anger while describing her. I didn't like his expressions at all but I felt sympathy for him at the same time. It was like he was the only one talking for an hour & I was the listener. All I was allowed to say is 'hmm' & 'oh'. He just wanted to make sure that I am listening attentively.

"Uma slept with several guys, when I came to know I got upset but I had forgiven her", he said.

"Why would she do such a thing?", I asked.

"I don't know Zara but she cheated on me several times."

"Oh.."

"But once I told Uma I have lost all my money, she left me."

"That's sad."

"But I did not stop there Zara, I followed her everywhere to **convince her but** her parents kept driving me away."

"If she cheated on you, left you for your silly prank, then for what joy you kept following her?"

He coughed, as if he got choked & replied, "You will not be able to understand."

I wanted to interrupt again because it was really confusing, she was at fault, so why was he trying to convince her? Many thoughts were going on in my mind.

"Can you expl...?"

"What would you like to order Zara?" He didn't let me complete my question & instantly changed the topic.

"Just iced tea."

"Eat something", he insisted with a smile.

"No, just the beverage would be fine", I smiled back.

He ordered chicken tandoori & literally stuffed it inside my mouth.

First meeting and showing so much care – I thought & kept smiling.

3.3

The next day he wanted to meet, but I felt it's too early meeting someone back to back like this so I denied. But we spoke over the phone all day long.

He kept asking me to meet so I made it up by speaking to him.

He insisted on a video call, I agreed.

When I accepted the call I saw a big smile on his face. Now this smile & the happiness in his eyes was created by me and was only for me. His face said it all.

That night he started flirting but I kept friend zoning him thinking it's too early. It was my semester break, I had a lot of free time so I didn't mind talking to him.

His words demanded my company, his eyes longed my presence.

It was becoming very difficult to stick to my 'Just Friends' category. He was the kind to be wanting companionship for twenty-four hours a day. I wanted the same.

We soon met again, he looked into my eyes & I looked down. I just couldn't do eye contact at all. I felt so shy I wanted the floor to break open so I could just dive into it. He kept looking. I excused myself, rushed to the bathroom and covered my face with my hands. I was so shy I couldn't even look at myself in the mirror.

I knew he was going to propose me today after all the romantic songs he dedicated to me last night.

I could literally feel the cupid hitting me really hard.

I mustered the courage, went back to the table and gave him a confident smile.

The ring was already on the table. And I was like - Oh my god! I really didn't know what to say, how to react, to smile or cry, or hug him or just do a handshake.

I told him, "I need time."

He said, "I can't give you time. You have to be mine, now."

I sat puzzled, I didn't know what to say, but proposing under pressure? Now, what kind of style is that?

I explained to him I needed more time to know him but he insisted on a 'yes' on the spot.

I was about to say no but his eyes already became teary.

I said "Yes." He was my first love. My first attraction.

I wasn't sure about this decision but I already said yes. I was actually worried what made him so impatient. But I also didn't want to lose him by saying no. I had started getting attached to him.

3.4

Days went by. We spoke to each other 24*7. He didn't leave me for a minute and neither did I want to be without him. He was the one making all plans,from forcing me to meet daily, to be on video call all night. I hesitated but he would compel me to agree.

He never made me regret listening to him. He always kept me happy.

His eyes had some sort of magic, I could look into his eyes for hours, fall into them so deep and drown.

Right after 4 days of being in a relationship Saif would regularly tell me "Zara let's get married,we won't inform anyone now,just 2 friends of mine will be there to witness it"

"What is the need for this,we will get married after a year with everyone present."

"No. Let's do it now.By chance something goes wrong",he said.

"There's no chance for by chance" I assured him.

It was the time for him to go back for his project in another city for 2 months. In just less than 2 weeks, we became inseparable souls.

After 2-3 days, we started missing each other, we were longing each other's company. He planned on coming back soon. The date finally arrived. I was so excited to see him. He was coming back. Just for me. I felt like the most loved girlfriend ever. I was so lucky to have him.

I decided to give him a surprise welcome at the airport.

I hired a guitarist who sung romantic songs right outside his arrival gate for 15-20 minutes, red carpet on which he walked, party planners who held banners & balloons for his welcome.

A middle-aged couple came to us and said, "We travel a lot but we haven't seen anything special like this in any of the airports, this is really sweet"

I started blushing. Saif gave me a smile.

I wanted everyone out there in the airport to know how special he was to me & how lucky I was to be his. He was also overwhelmed.

I was so excited that he was back. In just a few days of being in different cities, we both realised we couldn't live a moment without each other.

In the first week of our meeting only he introduced me to his parents and clearly told them that he wanted to marry me. Both agreed and looked happy with his decision. Now he wanted to meet my mom after coming back.

My mom knew we were friends, she had no clue at all that we were seeing each other. She liked him, but she never thought of us as a couple, maximum she could assume us to be besties. We decided to give her a surprise very soon and tell her we want to get married after a year after completing our studies.

Whenever I used to speak to Saif over the phone, he always made sure that I spoke to mom about him and praise about him daily, he enjoyed it.

My mom started to feel little curious as I never discussed any male friend with her before. Maybe it was Saif's style of giving her hints but still, she could only assume us to be good friends. But I was sure she would certainly accept him without a doubt. He was very lovable.

3.5

Saif & I kept meeting regularly. He always had the habit of checking my phone.

"You know Saif you are the first person I am actually allowing to handle my phone otherwise I am really not comfortable with letting anyone even glance at it for a second"

"Get used to it, I have the habit of doing it", Saif replied.

"Habit?"

"Yeah."

I didn't ask him anything. It was understood he did it with his exes. I was not liking it at first but there was nothing to hide so I just let him browse through it. I wanted him to feel happy.

"You know Uma always had her last seen hidden from all apps", he said while he was still going through my phone.

I realised even I had it off since years.

"Wait", I took the phone from his hand and made my last seen visible.

He was so happy, he smiled like a baby and hugged me.

We were sitting together in a restaurant, suddenly he asked for my phone again. He was going through the gallery and saw some old screenshot of a guy's texts but there was no reply from my end.

Saif got frantic, started yelling at me, he saw there was no reply & the texts were more than a year old. He started misbehaving with me. We had our movie in the next 5 minutes. We entered the multiplex.

"Don't be angry, there is nothing to feel upset about"

"Zara I am not liking it."

"Not liking what?"

"Just not liking it Zara"

He angrily threw the popcorn on the floor.

I was shocked. Not used to anyone behaving like this.

"I want to go home", I said with a broken voice

"You think I am going to let you go?"

He was angry and trying to show love at the same time. I was not being able to understand. But whatever it might be, there was nothing to behave like that.

We both had made a pact a day before, actually he was the one to imply these rules. So I said even you have to follow the same. It went on like this-

"You will not speak to any guy, not go out with your entire college group-just girls allowed, no interaction with any guy in college or gym, no male friends or cousins should be replied to."

I was ok with it as I thought I didn't need anyone apart from him. I was actually happy he is being so possessive.

3.6

We went for spa. He was going through the spa list and he asked the receptionist, "What would be best?"

She flirtingly smiled at him and said, "Body massage like the last time sir."

I looked at him. He told me he never had body massage done by female therapists. Why did he have to lie unnecessarily? He got caught here.

He started having a proper conversation with her, which lasted several minutes. They were laughing, flirting, smiling.

Saif wanted me to stay away from any guy, even if he was in 10th grade & here he was flirting away with that witchy female in front of me.

Soon he realised what he was doing and started to apologize. I was upset. This was the third week of our relationship.

Next day we met at a hookah lounge. Both spent a nice evening together. He dropped me home and left for a night out with his friend.

"I am going to a nightclub Zara."

"Okay"

He was at the nightclub for around 2 hours with no calls in between. It was Thursday night.

He called me once he left from there. I also didn't disturb him, gave him space. I always gave him space which I didn't know he was always misusing.

On Saturday night, while speaking to him over the phone, he received somebody's call on another phone at 2 am & asked that person to call him back after 20 minutes.

I asked, "Who was on the line?"

"Nobody. Just wrong number."

"You just asked the person to call you back?"

He confidently gave me the number knowing I would never call. He knew I trusted him blindly.

But I was already anxious after the receptionist episode. I called in that number and surprisingly it was a girl's voice.

"Hello."

"Hey."

"May I know why did you just call Saif?"

"We met at the pub on Thursday night, he asked me to call him today so I did"

"Oh"

"Who are you?"

"His girlfriend, and you?"

"I am Tiya".

"Are you sure about meeting him?"

"Definitely" She passed on the phone to another girl who confirmed and said he wanted her to call maybe they are supposed to meet tomorrow.

Instantly it clicked on my mind that he was planning on another night out on Sunday. I checked her profile and she looked like the girl guys pick up at night and have fun.

I just made it clear to Saif that I didn't want to be with him. I couldn't handle betrayal.

3.7

I couldn't sleep all night. In the morning I went to the balcony and saw his car.

I quickly removed my phone from airplane mode and read his messages.

In some, he said, "it's a trap, somebody was trying to cause problems between us."

It was not. The next few read that he was sorry and it won't happen again, the rest said that he would jump from the bridge or have pills. Now that shocked me.

I received a call from unknown number "Zara, I have been waiting all night outside your house, please come down and speak to me."

I was startled. He was waiting all night. Just for me. This relationship was completely new to me. I was never so close to anyone before. I went down to see him.

He was crying and saying sorry. My heart started beating faster. I couldn't see him like this.

"Last chance Zara, have mercy on me."

"Hmm"

"Please princess", he hugged me & cried.

I cried too.

He promised never to repeat it again. I believed him. Suddenly his phone flashed a message with a girl's pic which read – Are you coming tonight?

I had nothing to say after this. He said people are trying to cause a breakup between us. He forcibly gave me his phone to keep the entire day to go through it and observe it. He had 2 phones just like me.

I came back home, opened message, just one day before our first date there was a conversation with a girl called Hifa which went like-

Saif : Princess I will cut my wrist for you, please talk to me.

Hifa : It's over.

Saif : No it's not, I am waiting outside your place, meet me now or else I am coming up.

Hifa : No. Go away.

Saif : I love you princess.

OH MY GOD. What did I just read. He was dying for a girl just a day before he met me. How many princesses did he have?

I went through his Facebook messenger, both of us already had each other's passwords as he had emotionally blackmailed me for it once. I never opened his account. He did several times.

There was this chat with a girl named Asma 3 months ago which went on like-

Asma : Missed you baby.

Saif : Can't wait to see you again.

Asma : Can you get me those Cartier sunglasses we looked at today.

Saif : Certainly princess.

Woah! Princess number 2 just arrived. Saif understood I started to explore his phone and I was constantly disconnecting his calls.

Then I looked at his contacts which had several names stored as – Soul , Life , Soul 2 , Doll , Z , Z sis,U, U friend etc. I started to hate him now. But that was not enough. He called my mother "mom" but to my surprise, there were around 40-45 moms on his phone with name's like Angel's mom, Mom, Mumma, Mummy, Mummy new, Mummy new 2, Soul's mom, Doll's mom.

He was a son to almost half the moms in the city. That's great. It was his technique to get close to all the moms first to impress their daughters.

I went through his mail 'sent' category. I saw few mails sent to Uma with their pictures, some at a hotel room, some at his bedroom.

He wrote to her in mail –

"Uma I am really sorry for hitting you, I will never misbehave with you, you are my life, my heart. I will never enter your house forcefully again, I will never abuse your parents."

I couldn't believe what I just read. He seemed to be so well behaved it felt just impossible for anyone to believe what his true nature was. Even I couldn't believe it. But yes, it was nothing like people were trying to cause a breakup between us like he said it's a trap when Tiya called. Those girls who kept calling him or texting him were actually hanging out with him alone.

If he wanted to get married to me impatiently within a week of being together then I was sure he must be doing the same with his ex girlfriends also.

He gave me lame excuses. Which totally seemed false. He tried to send his best friend Kamir to persuade me to meet him, I denied. But while speaking to him over the phone I cross checked with him regarding the names I had seen in the phone, he agreed to all.

"Saif I am sending my staff with your phone outside, collect it and never come back", I told him.

"Give me a chance to explain Zara."

"No"

"I will stand outside your building all day, all night, until you come and see me. Neither will I eat or drink anything", he cried

"You do these tactics with everyone", I said and switched off my phone.

After 6 hours I switched it on to find hundreds of messages from him. He called and said, "Zara I am not feeling well, I am all alone, I don't have the strength to drive, there is no water in my car, I have hurt my leg, I think I am fainting, for the sake of humanity come and help me."

I immediately ran downstairs to help him but as he made me sit in his car he smiled. I understood it was a lie. I insisted on going back home, he took the car somewhere deserted & asked me to get down. He said, "I am going to burn down the car now along with myself in it. Please leave Zara." He took out kerosene and lighter from under the back seat.

I lost track of words. I couldn't say anything. I didn't know what to do. I tried my best to stop him.

The argument ended with us coming back together, his endless apologies, tears made me question my decision to leave him. He wanted to be with me. He wanted me badly.

"I have made a lot of mistakes in the past Zara, they all broke my heart, some used me for money, some for time pass, some mocked me. It was not my fault. I will not do anything like that with you. Zara, you are my baby, my princess. How can you think I am going to do anything of that sort to you. I will never betray you or hurt you."

3.8

We went to a party with friends after 3 days, there was a girl called Anu , we both didn't know her but she was with us in the group. Saif was flirting with her in front of me. I was not liking it. I didn't say anything, just asked him to drop me home.

I was not allowed to even reply to a "hi" to guys whom I called my brothers. I stopped all my outings with friends. He would always ask me to keep my phone on hold at home 24*7, even when I went out with my female friends. At first, I felt it's his love, concern, and possessiveness. But he deprived me of privacy, even when I would be at class he wanted me to keep my phone on & him on hold. When I opened my facebook, I saw my friend list reduced from 500 to 400. I didn't add strangers. But he removed 100 friends from my account without even asking me once. He didn't even allow me to accept any friend request from male friends, even if they were my classmates. He would decline them without even my knowledge. I changed my facebook password. Immediately his call came.

I asked him about my reduced friend list, he said "You don't need them."

"What do you mean by that?"

"Why will any guy be in your friend list Zara?"

I got really pissed off with him, he was flirting with girls and ruling my life here. I told him, "I am logging on your facebook now."

"Sure", he replied.

The first notification blinked.

"Anu accepted your friend request."

Newsfeed showed-

"Tiya changed her profile picture."

When I browsed through her pictures, I saw his likes on almost all and he claimed not to know her.

Another newsfeed showed me the picture of the spa receptionist he was speaking to.

Then there was another notification from his ex Hifa.

All were in his friend list, his exes, the girl he just met at the party, the ones he flirted with. Everyone was there. Then I realised that he would always keep a track of me by keeping my phone on hold so he could find ways to meet somebody else in between.

"Why don't you remove thousands of girls whom you dont even know from your friend list Saif?"

"I will"

"Now"

"No. Let it be. You add them back."

It was so easy for him to say this now. He didn't want to remove any of his girlfriends from his account but he removed my friends, when I asked him to do the same, just to skip doing that he told me to add my friends back.

Hats off to him.

He didn't give me any freedom but did whatever he wanted, with or without my knowledge. He didn't let me have any male friends, I didn't need anybody also, I just wanted him. But he had a huge group of female friends or did casual dating while being in a relationship with me.

He didn't like even a text coming to me from my friends. He always wanted me to keep my call on so he could hear whatever I am doing or talking about but he never did the same. He never gave me a moment of freedom but took his time off for hours whenever he wanted to.

He even wanted me to cut off with my female friends and relatives.

He didn't like me going out with anyone apart from him. It would sound good if he also did the same. He went out with his friends everyday but allowed me to meet my girlfriends not more than once in 2 weeks or maybe 3 weeks, that too for not more than an hour.

He went out with his female friends alone, met his cousins, went to family gatherings but he hated it when I even went to attend weddings.

He wanted to keep me away from my friend and family circle but didn't compromise with his for even half a day.

He would tell me he loves me that's why he is making me do this, he doesn't want anyone else to get my attention. But he was giving everyone attention.

He would tell me whom to talk to or not talk to.

I was thinking it's love and possessiveness but my friends made me realise this is not healthy in a relationship. These signs were not good.

None of these rules implied to him, he was a free bird but I was a bird in his cage.

He understood I wanted to leave him, he said "I am going to come up to your place now."

"You are not allowed to", I said.

"Who will stop me?", he angrily said.

"You say this to every girl you date. I will not let you come up to my home ever as I know you always threaten all your girlfriends of entering their place."

It was his fault, he understood he was wrong, he got caught and was trying to overpower me. I did not speak to him for days, again saw him waiting outside my house crying.

He said, "I am sorry, it won't happen again."

I gave him another chance, I loved him.

3.9

I noticed several times Saif was very irresponsible towards his mother. In fact, he never answered her calls, didn't talk to her while he was at home, didn't eat with her, didn't pay attention to her. He always answered back to her rudely.

I taught him the importance of mother, I requested him to take her out on outings, speak to her with respect, ask her with concern about her health and what she needed.

He would always misbehave with her and whenever he did, I didn't speak to him.

So for me, he started respecting her, he took her out, he spoke to her politely and I made sure he did that. I always wanted the blessing of his mother to be with us.

His mother complained about him wherever she went, it felt little odd because she made it very obvious. She sometimes said he hits her, I really couldn't believe this, he didn't seem like that, he was like a prince. But at heart, I was afraid. If it actually turned out to be true then what would he do later.

He always called me his princess, treated me like one at times, showered me with love all the time. He really made me feel special and always made me feel wanted. I always wanted somebody like that. He didn't leave me alone. He filled up all the empty space I had in my life.

The best part about him was his eyes. I always told him "Your eyes have magic" and he smiled back.

For me, the most important part of being in a relationship is being wanted and loved. I never wanted to be alone, he never left me alone. He was always on the phone with me or present with me.

He wanted to meet me daily but I could not. He got really upset whenever I couldn't meet him or he waited for hours outside my house until he convinced me to meet him.

Whenever we met, he showered me with his love.

I always asked him, "Are you real?"

He called me the love of his life, he said he had a really messed up past with his love life, several breakups, all ended terribly, nothing lasted more than 2-3 months he said.

My past was nothing, he was the first man in my life. I had male friends, dated one also but it couldn't be called a relationship.

With Saif, being the first one in my life, I was little inexperienced as I didn't know how to handle a guy. I gave him full liberty, listened to whatever he said and tried my best to keep him happy.

There was something I didn't like about him, his impatience. He would get impatient for everything. I always wanted time for everything but he just couldn't give me time.

My life starting revolving around him. He was my world.

He loved me because he said I was obedient and I respected him.

But he was not loyal, he always made mistakes, accepted it later, repented for his mistakes and again repeated. He got offensive also when I accused him of them.

He always wanted to show everyone that I was his girl, he put up our pictures on social media from his and my profile. He was an ideal boyfriend-it seemed to everyone.

I just asked him for 3 things-

1. Respect,

2. Love,

3. Loyalty.

He couldn't be loyal. I gave him a lot of time to change but it wouldn't just happen. He would respect me in front of others but when we were alone he would overpower me every time. He would monitor everything that I did, tried to dominate me, always wanted to do what he did, controlled me, choose whom I spoke to, kept an update of every minute – All these were applicable to me only, nothing was applicable to him.

He sometimes misbehaved with me also, especially for not allowing him to touch me. He was the first person I was actually so close to, he should have respected that. There should have been some sort of understanding which was completely absent. He always wanted to make out, I would deny or push him away and there would be an outburst from him.

I just wanted time, he lacked patience. He should have handled me with care, at least thought these things are new to me. But he always wanted everything, right now.

No delays, no excuses, no waiting.

3.10

Whenever I ignored him he would speak to me through my mom. He impressed her with his sweet, caring words. He showed her how much he cared for me, how he could not live without me. He assured her that he would take care of me life long and never break my heart.

My mom also started liking him. She saw how madly he was in love with me, how he couldn't live without me, how he waited for hours just to see me. She loved him like her own son. She always wanted a son in her son in law and she found it in him. She was convinced that nobody is going to love me more than him.

I didn't tell anything negative about him to anyone, not even mom. I only discussed his positive side. Mom didn't know about his rowdy behavior.

One day I found out he took pictures of us while we were very close and I didn't know it. I really got mad at him for this. I didn't speak to him for a week.

He really tried to convince me, sent his friends home just to make up, waited outside my home everyday just to say sorry.

I knew I shouldn't continue my relationship with him, he had done too much this time, but my heart became soft seeing him in this condition. I just couldn't see him cry. Seeing his tears was my biggest weakness.

Once we met at a hookah lounge, and had a fight over some topic.

"Why can't you listen to me?"

"I always listen to you Saif."

"Yes, But why not this?"

"You want me to again put up pictures with you when you already did it last week?"

"Yeah, Why not?", he replied.

He took my phone, added our picture again.

"Now it's better and don't you dare delete it" he said.

"Why the hell are you speaking to me like that?"

"Because I am the man."

"I know you are my man but there is a certain way to behave Saif."

"You don't teach me how to behave."

He dragged me by my hand and made me sit in his car forcibly. I kept quiet. He kept pinning me and asked me why I was quiet.

"Zara speak up."

"We should remain silent if angry."

"No. Your silence is killing my mood. Speak up."

I was not saying anything.

He drove the car really rashly.

"Speak now."

"I am not liking this behavior of yours."

He drove faster.

I tried to calm him down by holding his hand, he pushed me instead.

He lost his cool, he didn't realise what he had done, it really hurt me hard. Then he realised he made a mess.

"You will leave me now Zara?"

"My head is hurting Saif, I think it's bleeding."

"You will leave me."

Please check whether it's bleeding or not. He then realised he accidentally hurt me hard. He checked it, it wasn't bleeding he said but it was swollen badly.

"I will not drop you home."

"I want rest Saif."

"No you are not going back home, tell the world you will marry me now, put it on facebook."

"Give me medicines at least."

He got few medicines and tried to care for me but it wasn't enough. It was paining like hell.

"I want to go home, let me go."

He didn't want to let go of me, he thought I would complain but I never would.

He put the glass up, locked the car and snatched my phone, "You are not going anywhere."

I felt trapped.

"Please let me go."

Somehow I managed to go home after that but promised to meet him tomorrow only to ensure he let me go that moment.

He called me and I found out that he is playing tennis.

He hurt my head, instead of being concerned he was playing tennis.

I lay down on my bed and when I removed the pillow I saw blood. My head was still bleeding. I told him but he said, "You have to meet me tomorrow"

That's all he cared about, whether I am in pain, dead, alive, half dead – It didn't matter to him. He just wanted to meet.

I was too nervous to talk about it at home but in the night the pain grew harder. I went to take a shower and could see blood on the floor.

When he pushed me, I was wearing a big hair clip which broke on my head, the clutches of it had pierced through my head and caused injury.

I told him I wanted to leave him but he didn't accept I was breaking up.

I told my mom about this incident as the pain was getting unbearable. She couldn't believe Saif could do such a thing. She took me to the hospital on time. Luckily, it wasn't too late, it got cured.But I broke up with him.

He was just not listening to me, he was not leaving me alone.

The words of his mother was buzzing in my head that he used to hit her. I understand he pushed me by accident but why didn't he bang his head in anger.

3.11

He followed me everywhere, literally everywhere. The moment I stepped out of my house, I could see him sitting in his car. His car followed my car all the time. So many times I made him understand that I need time but he just wouldn't give me time.

I loved him, my head still hurt, I would always think about him, I wanted to be with him but I was too scared. He hurt me that day, it was due to his insecurity of losing me, but he hurt me.

I was about to start talking to him in a few days but I kept telling him I need time. One day he got his mom to convince me to start talking to him again. I really respected his mom and loved her until that day. I was the one who kept requesting him to love her instead of being harsh towards her. But that day I realised I was wrong.

She said, "For Zara, Saif left his studies, he has become dark standing in the sun, he is keeping his door locked at night while speaking to her."

Keeping door locked? I thought. I didn't question her. I kept quiet. She was elder to me, most importantly she was his mom. I had to respect her.

Every word of Saif's mother hit me like an arrow. During our relationship she kept saying that there has been a lot of improvement in Saif after I have come into his life, that he has started staying at home at night rather than club hopping, she said he started giving her more time, she said nobody could be a better match than me.

Don't couples need privacy? She wanted to monitor whatever he spoke to me and be a part of it.

She found me at fault. My fault according to her was –Breaking up with him and not wanting to be with him.

Didn't his mom have the sense to understand that her son had hurt me earlier that's why I was ignoring Saif.

Saif and I both loved each other a lot. Nothing could come between us. But his mom's words drew a big line between both of us.

Being my mom's only child, her daughter's choice was very dear to her.

I understood his mom would always come between us and I didn't want him to leave her. So I left Saif, for the sake of his mom.

3.12

His mom called me one day and said, "Saif has made my life hell, he is not right for you, threaten him and insult him everytime he follows, stop talking to him, he is mistreating me also, he will make your life hell after marriage."

Saif kept following me wherever I went. I was sympathizing seeing the efforts he put in but I had to shout at him just to follow his mom's advise because she knew her son best.

A few days later he went to see Jemina for marriage along with his mother. He came back the next day, again followed me. I got really irritated. He was dating so many girls, seeing few girls for marriage and here he was trying to convince me.

What does he want? Why can't he take a stand? He said he loved me so why would he date other girls?

I was very adamant this time, I ignored him for months, didn't respond to his calls as per his mother's advice. She asked me to insult, ignore, let him mature. I did the same, thinking he would change.

He didn't stop following me.

"I don't want to marry you Saif. I am not comfortable with the idea of being cheated over and over again. Please go"

"I will not go Zara."

Seeing the effort he put in for months and months and the amount of tears he shed for me, my heart melted. I just couldn't see him crying. My mom loved him dearly, she thought he would be the best son in law, madly in love with her daughter. But she was unaware of what Saif had been doing to me.

I really loved him. I gave him another chance.

Soon, he did something really unruly outside my house, I got upset with him.

Again the same thing started – Following, apologising, crying. He kept on making mistakes in the process, said sorry and I kept on forgiving him. I sympathized with him. Saif knew me too well, he knew I would get convinced seeing him cry or seeing him ill. He won my heart again. I started speaking to him again.

3.13

Saif was unaware that his friend's wife who acted to know nothing about me in front of him would regularly call me to complain about him.

She pretended to be a guide to Saif so that he started trusting her.

"Don't trust him, he is worthless", she said.

I was very disappointed by whatever she told me. I wanted to leave the country. I even started making the preparations to study abroad but as Saif came to know about it, he went mad with anger. He would never let me go anywhere.

I never complained about him to anyone, not even my own parents.

Again she called me one day and said he is dating other girls.

I was very hurt that he was still doing the same thing. I wanted him to feel the pain of betrayal so I spoke to him about few hypothetical guys who didn't even exist.

I even went to another city and met Zaroon in a mall for an hour. Zaroon's formal proposal had come for marriage a few months back.

My mom didn't like the fact that I was doing this to Saif, she said, "You know he is very sensitive and he is over possesive about you, you don't have to do what he did, just forgive him and give him a chance."

"No mom. He has not stopped. He is still cheating on me."

I forced her to accompany me. She had no other option.

I kept telling her if his mom can do it several times, why couldn't she do it at least once for me.

Zaroon was a perfect prospective. I just cared about clicking a few pictures with him and keeping it stored on my phone as Saif had the habit of checking it everytime he could.

I chose Zaroon because Saif already knew about the proposal and just by listening to it he lost his cool so there wouldn't have been any other way out to make him feel the same.

Saif was at his best behavior. He was showing improvement. I thought of giving him a final chance. I didn't want to hurt him. I was really impressed by all the effort he put in for me.

24*7 he would wait outside my house, just to follow me so he could convince me when I had already made it clear I didn't want to marry him long back. But he showed that he loved me. He just wasn't giving up on me.

I like people who don't give up easily, he showed everyone how much he loved me.

3.14

I joined the university in the same city, just like Saif wanted. I loved him a lot and I believed I could change him. I started making preparations for giving him a surprise party on our first meeting anniversary date. I kept it a secret, both of us loved giving each other surprises. I didn't even let him get the slightest idea about it. I planned on inviting several guests including his relatives and friends a week ahead of the party, e-cards were ready.

I bought a lovely platinum bracelet, beautifully designed chain, mom got him a villa with a personal pool, a designer suit from his favourite premium brand.

One day I was at a restaurant with my friend and suddenly he came and took me along forcibly. He was behaving very strangely. I understood he's become frustrated waiting for me past few months. I thought I will be able to calm him down and then go back home. But the situation got worse.

He wanted to marry me forcefully. I told him I would marry him, give me some time. He denied. He just didn't listen. Not even in my nightmare, I could imagine Saif to behave like that. I was in shock. I cried a lot.

He didn't let me speak to anyone, took away my phone and said he would never let me go back home.

"Do or die Zara."

"Do what?"

"Marry me right now or I will kill you."

"I love you, I will marry you. Please give me some time, you are still having affairs."

"No. Marry me right now."

After seeing this behavior of his, I didn't disclose about the party next month.

"Call your mother and tell her right now that you will never come back."

"No."

"Say you want to run away with me."

"Why run away Saif, everyone will accept you."

"Zara say you are running with me."

"Saif, please. I love you, idiot. I am not going anywhere leaving you. But I want everything to happen properly."

I would have married him that night if he wouldn't have misbehaved with me.

"I will shoot you Zara, marry me right now."

I asked him to call mom he just wouldn't. After few hours he did call her. Both tried our best to ensure he dropped me home but he didn't.

His mom was with us, she saw what was happening but she couldn't do much. Maybe she didn't want to do much. Seeing me in this condition, she could have done a lot of things. She knew any girl would leave Saif after what he did.

My mom called her and said, "They are getting engaged next month, why is he rushing. Even if he wants to, he can do it with everyone's blessings."

His mom said, "Zara is crying a lot. He is misbehaving with her. You should get her back,why don't you threaten Saif ? "

Saif called few friends and told them he is eloping with me, one of them informed my mom that I am in trouble and told many disturbing things about him. My mom got more tensed.

Saif just kept on pressurizing me. I couldn't believe he was the same person I fell in love with. I just couldn't stop crying. He was my prince in shining armor and this is what he ended up doing. Some wounds are not visible but they have a very strong impact on the mind. The worst part is that he doesn't even realize what he is doing.

His parents had no control over him. Maybe they didn't try enough. They knew their son. I had full love and respect for his parents. Why didn't they stop Saif from traumatizing me that night if I was their daughter. They knew everything.

His mother had held the holy book a few months back and promised to love me like her daughter that is why I believed her. His dad also promised that he will take the responsibility for my safety. What happened to all these promises that night?

3.15

His behavior got worse as time passed, he was out of control. I wasn't feeling well at all, somehow I managed to take him to the hospital, called my mom also.

I was too weak to explain what he did with me. Neither did I want to. I saw many messages and calls on her phone from his friends saying that I was in danger with him. That is why mom was worried all night about me.

I was feeling dizzy, I called my family members. Everyone present there were only concerned about my health, they didn't know what happened the previous night. They were taking me home to call my family doctor but on the way, innumerable calls & messages came from Saif's friends whom he had called the previous night he was with me. They called on my mom's phone to warn her from unknown numbers which my dad received and read. They requested my parents not to reveal their names as they said - Saif is a bully, a spoilt brat, he would harm their family & kids.

Saif's father complained that Saif is going out of hand, he is being unable to handle him.

Also, my staff, Jia called and said she was raped by Saif and she was crying for help, she knew my father was there but she didn't stop. My dad heard this also. First call from his friends, then this staff. My dad was shocked and disgusted .

Immediately after that strict actions were taken against him. He got arrested. But I knew Saif always makes mistakes in anger, blames me even if it's not my fault, realises his mistake later and apologizes. I knew he wouldn't have realised what he is doing back then but as usual, his realization will awaken. I couldn't see him in this condition. We decided to ease out on things immediately.

My mom couldn't see her precious prince in this condition from the very first day. She knew him well that he makes mistakes in his impatience. She tried her best to protect him.

In the movie Veer Zara, it's not Veer's fault but he keeps quiet just for the sake of Zara's honour. But Saif was not Veer. It was his fault, his friends were ruining our relationship past few weeks by informing about his affairs, but still, he found fault in me. The worst part was that he lied. He could have accepted & said it's his fault, "I'm sorry" -like always but he didn't. Instead, he started talking ill about me to everyone.

Before the next hearing, Jia again came running to my home. She said, "Saif had raped me several times", she handed over her phone to me showing me the call log between her & Saif.

She said, "he would rape her & forcibly take out information about my whereabouts." Jia begged my mom to save her & said she wanted to file a complaint against him for rape. But mom refused doubting Jia was lying.

On the other hand, many things were wrongly said on his defense by his lawyers. This is their profession.

He and his father tolerated this? Real men don't even bear hearing such rubbish against their wife or daughter in law no matter what.

I never asked him for anything monetary, neither a single present nor any favours as I myself belong to a very wealthy family. I have always been spoilt with love & gifts from all my family members.

In reality, he always forced me to marry him, I kept asking time for him to mature. I would deny any present he gave me or maybe select the most reasonable one. Saif always praised me for this nature, he said that's why he loved me because I was not like his ex-girlfriends. I never made him spend his money even though he always wanted to.

My mom wanted his release, she always said he had an innocent heart & he was like her son. She requested my father to reduce the pressure to prevent his bail from getting cancelled. Soon he was out.

Even after coming out, he didn't have the balls to say the truth or accept his mistake. He did a lot of things previously which was worth complaining but I didn't. I didn't do anything against him since a year. That night he crossed all limits. If he truly loved me , he wouldn't have done what he did that night.

3.16

He was still sending me lovey-dovey messages to patch up. Again his friends updated me about him. I hated when they called me, they said he was already too busy looking out for girls.

This is what his mom always wanted. She very well knew I would leave him after that night, that is why she let him misbehave with me, complained about him to my mom.

Saif told me when we were together that he hated his mom because she caused most of the break ups between him and his girlfriends. He also told me that they spoke ill about her.

But I was the one who always insisted that he took care of his mom. Several times when there were men working at his place, he would leave his mom alone to look after the work done but as I came to know this I made sure she was not left alone with strangers. I still don't understand what is her problem.

Saif wanted me to stay single, still sending heartbroken messages to me but he himself was sending proposals in many places. Again history repeats. He was still calling me – his girl and my mom – Mumma but simultaneously also creating a new family somewhere else along with his parents like always- New mom, new dad, new sister, new girl.

And here I was sitting like a dumbo, lost in his love, rejecting the best of proposals. Then why was he wasting his time here, he didn't need me I just wished the best for him.

I was fooled enough. I knew he was cooking stories like always and cheating on me again. Not anymore. If this was not "Veer Zara" for him, it was not for me also. Saif couldn't be Veer how did he expect me to be like Zara.

First Jemina, then I found some other girl's clothes in his car, then some duet love songs which he was singing with another girl were on his phone. These were few instances of his cheating while I was in a relationship with him and he expected me to forgive him each time. I did forgive him. I loved him. But he kept cheating on me. I wanted him to know why I was running away from him so I met Zaroon. There was no other way I could make him stop his affairs. He still knew I was his, just his. Still, he misbehaved. Zaroon was just a realization check for Jemina.

Saif knew I could stay alone for months only with the memories of the person I love.

My point is when you are already involved somewhere else why to lie again. Just be happy and stop bothering me.

4 people, 2 ex-lovers with different partners,2 different dates, same venue.

But still, I wouldn't do it until he did it. I knew he would be broken. If I cared so much about him in spite of being hurt and cheated, if this is not love then what is it.

This time also I would let him do whatever he wanted, then I would do the same. Not before. I know he won't be able to handle the pain what he put me through each time.

I broke all my rules for him. I loved him.

I fell in love with a loving, respectable, fearless, charming prince, not an unfaithful, liar and a hurting monster.

A good man will be honest no matter what, not hide behind lies and deceit. If he was already having fun somewhere why was he getting creepy seeing me happy. If I was not hindering his happiness, why was he blocking ways for me. He shouldn't have been unfair.

Saif was my pride. I had no pride left. It was crushed by my "man" and "caring in-laws" that night. So congratulations to him. He had nothing left to break.

I loved him because of the efforts he put in for me, but there were many reasons to leave him. The list grew longer now. He didn't leave me for a moment, didn't let me go anywhere so even I had held on to him.

He was like a detective for almost one year, he found out every detail about me, paid most of the guys outside my house to acquire information about me. He just didn't want to miss me for a second also. If he went to the bathroom or for having food, he would keep someone else waiting outside to follow me.

He asked for another chance but he was not sitting idle, he was dancing at parties, going to clubs, dating girls. He didn't get hospitalised in tension the way I got. He very well knew I could never see him in pain, I would go to him running. He wanted me to remain single while he was fooling around.

3.17

He made such strong promises that he would never break my trust or mistreat me. That's why I trusted him. Where did all the promises go? He made thousands of videos saying sorry and making promises, were those lies?

During the entire break up phase, I didn't meet any guy while Saif slept with uncountable women. He forced me to marry him and insulted me when I refused. Saif has no regret or sadness of losing his girl. He was saying sorry but he was not.

My mom believed - Saif would be completely faithful to me. No one can touch or harm me when he was with me. Both of us couldn't live without each other and this is what he did? My mom thought it was a love story made in heaven. She loved us both. Saif made so many false promises. Didn't his words have honor? She wasn't aware of the truth.

How can Saif forgive himself. How can he even look at himself in the mirror and not see what a huge blunder he has done. He lied to us all. My mom and I totally trusted him. Will God ever forgive him?

He had realized he was wrong. Like always, he started cursing himself for what he did.He felt really sorry. He loved me a lot he said. I was his princess & he had broken his princess. He realized his frustration led to hurting me, then he couldn't digest getting arrested so he spoke wrong about me. He wanted to die.

I would tell him when we were together if you are gone, who will take care of me, who will protect me? I said I needed my man by my side always. These words kept him alive. Every time he would make mistakes, fight, come back to me. I would fight & ignore. Both knew we would be together someday or the other.

But this time was different. He couldn't call his princess, he couldn't chase her, he couldn't cry in front of her, he couldn't show her his small wounds. He couldn't face her this time. He knew he was wrong. But he longed for her. He was trying to contact me daily.

I let him go. It was over for me. I didn't mind if he got married or got in a relationship with someone. I used to be extremely possessive about him, just like he was about me. But no longer. He could never be faithful. But what I was not liking it, that he didn't want me to get married and he said he would shoot himself if I did so.

Many thoughts were going on in my mind. Why did he get frustrated that day, even if he got frustrated why did he misbehave with me? Why didn't he cry like a baby hugging me like he used to? That's how I used to melt into his arms & listen to whatever he said. I had planned such a beautiful surprise for him, the presents were still lying in front of me, my email was popping reminders of sending the e-invite to the guests, I was getting calls from the hotel regarding the confirmation of catering & decoration theme, his suit was ready after alteration, I was imagining clasping the bracelet across his wrist & the chain around his neck. But at the same time, his friends told me he was already into other girls.

We always don't get whom we desire. Both wished the best for each other. Life has to go on.

When love becomes a lie, it's time to say goodbye.

———— ◆ ————

www.ingramcontent.com/pod-product-compliance
Lightning Source LLC
Chambersburg PA
CBHW030553130626
46552CB00006B/2536